SURVIVING THE IMPOSSIBLE

SURVIVING A ZOMBIE APOCALYPSE

CHARLIE OGDEN

Gareth Stevens
PUBLISHING

Please visit our website, **www.garethstevens.com**.
For a free color catalog of all our high-quality books,
call toll free 1-800-542-2595 or fax 1-877-542-2596.

CATALOGING-IN-PUBLICATION DATA

Names: Ogden, Charlie.
Title: Surviving a zombie apocalypse / Charlie Ogden.
Description: New York : Gareth Stevens Publishing, 2018. | Series: Surviving the impossible | Includes index.
Identifiers: ISBN 9781538214992 (pbk.) | ISBN 9781538214220 (library bound) | ISBN 9781538215005 (6 pack)
Subjects: LCSH: Zombies--Juvenile literature. | Survival--Juvenile literature.
Classification: LCC GR581.O43 2018 | DDC 398.21--dc23

Published in 2018 by
Gareth Stevens Publishing
111 East 14th Street, Suite 349
New York, NY 10003

Written by: Charlie Ogden
Edited by: Kirsty Holmes
Designed by: Matt Rumbelow

Photo credits: Abbreviations: l-left, r-right, b-bottom, t-top, c-center, m-middle. Images are courtesy of Shutterstock.com. With thanks to Getty Images, Thinkstock Photo and iStockphoto. Cover: bg – Nik Merkulov; hands – Alex Malikov; book – Leszek Glasner. 2 – eolintang. 3 – Andrey_Kuzmin. 4 – leolintang. 5: bg – Tyler Olson. 6 – Tithi Luadthong. 7 – pikselstock. 8 – Tajborg. 9 – Warpaint. 10: t – Dmytro Vietrov; b – Korionov. 11: bg – leolintang; front – Yellow Cat. 12: t – IfH; bl – XONIX. 13 – Kochneva Tetyana. 14 – Milosz_G. 15 – Taigi. 16 – photka. 17 – Tithi Luadthong. 18 – Pop Paul-Catalin. 19: tl – NIPAPORN PANYACHAROEN; tr – Alex Staroseltsev; tm – Ruslan Ivantsov; m – MAHATHIR MOHD YASIN. 19 – Lpuddori. 20 – Billion Photos. 21 – jakkapan. 22: bg – studioalef. Tr – Tithi Luadthong; bl – RobinE. 23: bg – Gehrke; Panacea Doll. 24: t – designbydx; br – Cristian Dina; bl – sunchick; studiovin. 25 – Jocortphotography. 26 – RikoBest. 27 – leolintang. 28: t – studiovin; b – Dmytro Vietrov. 30: bg – latino; br – cenker atila. .

Printed in China

CPSIA compliance information: Batch CW18GS: For further information contact
Gareth Stevens, New York, New York at 1-800-542-2595.

CONTENTS

Words that look like THIS can be found in the glossary on page 31.

THE OUTBREAK

Surviving a zombie apocalypse isn't easy. To get through it, you're going to need to be smart, fast, and willing to fight. Keeping your cool when the zombie outbreak first begins is crucial to surviving the apocalypse. This is the first challenge that you're going to have to face — you'd better be ready.

If a HORDE of zombies takes you by surprise, it will probably take you a few seconds to work out what is going on. This will be the first time that you ever see a zombie and, up until now, you probably never imagined they could ever be real. To stay alive, you're going to need to forget your fear and get out of there — fast! You can work out what's going on later. For now, you need to get to safety.

The worst way to find out that the zombie apocalypse has begun is when four or five scary, open-mouthed zombies attack you out of nowhere. It doesn't matter if they corner you on the street, try to force their way into your house at night, or storm into your math class while your teacher is explaining algebra — you've got to be ready, no matter what.

NEWS WARNING

If you're lucky, you'll hear about the zombie outbreak before they reach you. You're most likely to find out about the apocalypse by hearing it on the news. This will help you to get ready for your first zombie encounter. However, a news warning about the zombie apocalypse comes with its own risks.

If you've heard that the dead are coming back to life, then so has everyone else. It's not a secret that people can keep to themselves. Because of this, it's likely that everyone around you will go into SURVIVAL MODE. People in this state can be dangerous and will do whatever they have to in order to survive — make sure to stay out of their way and focus on what is important.

You should have time to find your loved ones before the zombies arrive. If you have your family and friends around you, the zombie apocalypse might not be completely horrific! So if you have time to prepare, take the chance to find the ones you love before the apocalypse begins!

HOW TO SPOT A ZOMBIE

When the panic starts and people are running in every direction, you'll only have a split second to work out if someone is a friendly human or a brain-hungry zombie! Learning how to spot a zombie is one of the first things you will need to know. It could mean the difference between life and death!

SKIN

One of the easiest ways to spot a zombie is by their skin. Zombies don't care about being shot, run over, or hit with a baseball bat. This means that most zombies will be badly beaten up and their skin will be bruised and bleeding.

EYES

However, you may not always be able to IDENTIFY a zombie by its skin. Some zombies manage to get by without losing any arms or cracking open their head. In these situations, your best chance at spotting a zombie is to look at their eyes. All zombies have cold, pale, BLOODSHOT eyes that stare right at you. Even if a person has only been a zombie for a few seconds, their eyes will give them away.

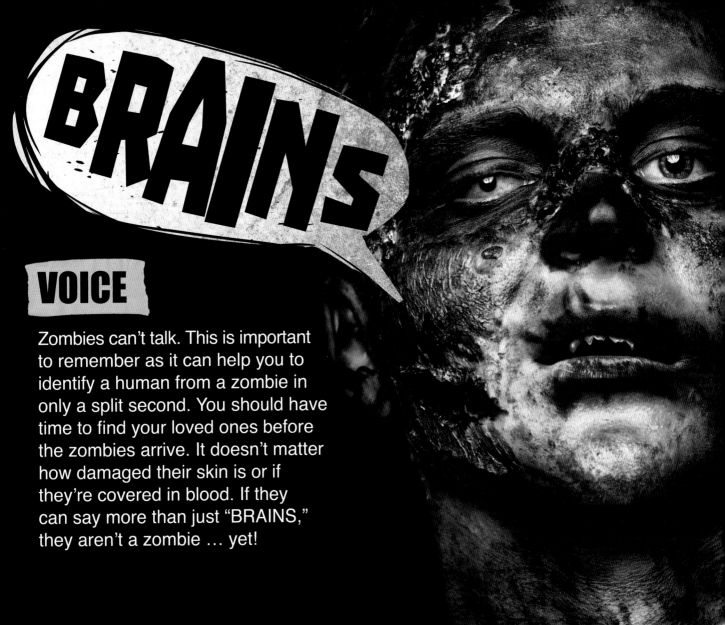

BRAINS

VOICE

Zombies can't talk. This is important to remember as it can help you to identify a human from a zombie in only a split second. You should have time to find your loved ones before the zombies arrive. It doesn't matter how damaged their skin is or if they're covered in blood. If they can say more than just "BRAINS," they aren't a zombie ... yet!

Take no chances and trust no one. Anyone could be INFECTED in a zombie apocalypse!

WALK

Possibly the most noticeable thing about zombies is the way they walk. Now, you might have watched movies or read comics in which zombies can run as fast as Olympic athletes. Lucky for you, this can't really happen. Zombie survivalists know that when a person turns into a zombie, their legs become stiff, their knees swell, and their GAIT is unstable. This makes slow shuffling a zombie's top speed.

The standard zombie will walk at an incredibly slow pace, often with one leg dragging behind the other. Make sure to use this to your advantage! If you see two or three zombies approaching over a hill — don't panic! You probably still have half an hour until they finally reach you. Maybe you should use that time to FORTIFY your zombie hideout?

CHOOSING A HIDEOUT

Once you've got away from any nearby zombies and are safe (at least for now), it's time to start thinking about creating a hideout. Without a decent BASE, you don't stand a chance of surviving in the zombie apocalypse for more than a few days.

Maybe not...

Some people have small bases that only have one way in and out. Examples of this type of base are attics, bomb shelters, and basements. Because these places are difficult to find and get into, people think that they make a good hideout. This is false. You can hide from the zombies for a while, but eventually the horde will find you. When they do, you don't want to be stuck in a basement with no way out.

Make sure that your base has windows and viewpoints so that someone can always be a LOOKOUT.

LOCATION, LOCATION, LOCATION

It doesn't matter if you find a hideout that is as strong as a castle — if it's in the wrong place, you'll end up dead anyway. The perfect location is somewhere near food and clean water and that doesn't have many infected people hanging around. Don't stop until you find a suitable location, such as a farm outside a town that has its own well. If you choose your hideout poorly, it could be the last mistake you ever make.

CLEARING YOUR HIDEOUT

When you finally find a suitable base — a place where you'll be safe, which you can really call home — you'll need to make sure that it is clear of the UNDEAD. Now, at this point in the apocalypse, you probably won't have many weapons and your zombie-fighting skills might not be up to scratch. Approach cautiously and carefully. If there are too many zombies inside, it's best to not risk it. Keep looking until you find somewhere else.

FORTIFYING YOUR HIDEOUT

Once you've found your perfect hideout and it is clear of all unwanted zombies, it is time to fortify your base so that it can withstand being attacked by the undead. Don't think that this won't happen — the zombies WILL find your hideout and they WILL try to get inside. The only question is, will you be ready?

Put fences up around your hideout. Trail barbed-wire around your PERIMETER. Board up every window and doorway (leaving a few exits open in case you need to escape, of course). Have people on lookout at all times. Keeping your hideout safe is one of the most important jobs in a zombie apocalypse — don't let your hideout be your downfall!

KNOW YOUR SURROUNDINGS

Once you have fortified your hideout and you are sure you'll be able to fend off any zombie attackers that might come your way, it is time to get to know your surrounding area. This can mean the difference between life and death, so make sure to take some paper with you and jot down some notes.

The best hideouts are those that are a little way outside of a town, because you can easily make runs into the town to get food, weapons, and other supplies. However, zombies tend to gather in towns. So make sure that your hideout is a good distance away, otherwise the zombies might come to you first!

In your nearby town, you need to know the location of the supermarket and hospital. The best towns will also have places to find weapons, tall buildings to look out from, and a fresh water supply. You should make a note of these places too. In an emergency, knowing where to get food, water, weapons, and medicine could save your life.

Top Tip: Do not try to take all the food and medicine in nearby towns back to your hideout. If you do, your hideout might become a TARGET. When other groups of survivors find out that you have all the food, they are going to want some — and they aren't going to ask nicely.

GATHERING SUPPLIES

You are going to spend a lot of time gathering supplies during the zombie apocalypse. However, this won't be like going to the grocery store with your friends to pick out candy and snacks. To survive the zombie apocalypse, you will need to always be on the lookout for things that can help you. If you know what supplies to look for, as well as the best ways to find them, then you might just make it through the zombie apocalypse.

CANNED FOOD

Depending on how long the zombie apocalypse has been going on, you will need to look for different types of food. To begin with, eat as much fresh food as you can, such as fruit, vegetables, meat, and bread. These foods will not stay fresh for long and no one will be stocking the supermarket with fresh produce anytime soon. This could be the last time you ever eat these foods.

After the first couple of weeks, your attention should turn to canned food. Canned foods can stay fresh for a number of years, making them the perfect food for surviving the zombie apocalypse. Canned peaches may not be as nice as actual peaches, but it's better than a diet of brains.

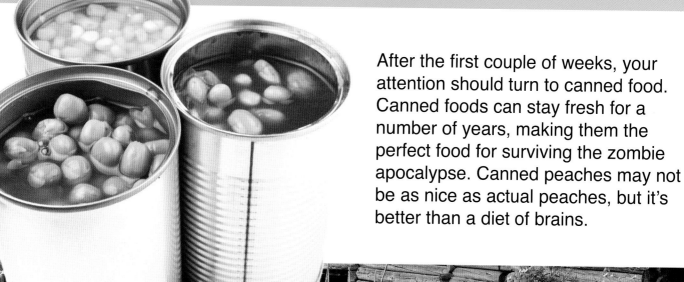

When you eat fresh fruits and vegetables, make sure to save any seeds you come across. With these, you could start growing your own fresh fruit.

MEDICINE

Medical supplies are very important in a zombie apocalypse. There is one problem though — most people don't know how to properly use medical supplies. Drinking the wrong medicine or swallowing the wrong pill could be as bad for you as having a zombie bite a chunk out of your arm.

The best way to get around this problem is by finding a doctor and convincing them to join your group. Until you have a doctor in your party, it is best to stick to what you know. Grab bandages, medical tape, anti-bacterial wipes, and anything else you think you might need. Also, make sure to collect any soap that you find. Washing regularly will help you to stay healthy and could save your life.

COMMUNICATIONS

After zombies take over the world, it won't be long before normal forms of communication stop working. There will be no people to deliver letters and no MAINS ELECTRICITY to power phones or computers. Finding devices that allow you to communicate with others will therefore be very valuable in the zombie apocalypse. Short-range walkie-talkies are what you want. These gadgets use batteries, so if you add these to your supply list as well, you will be able to stay in contact with your group at all times.

If you don't have any walkie-talkies, blowing a whistle can help you to contact your group from far away when you're in trouble.

WEAPONS AND TOOLS

While food and supplies are very important for surviving the zombie apocalypse, you won't get very far unless you have some weapons and tools as well.

Many people see heavy machine guns and finely-sharpened samurai swords as the ideal weapon to have in a zombie apocalypse — and they might be right. However, we should be realistic. Unless you already know where to find a machine gun or samurai sword, which would be quite unusual, it is unlikely that you will simply come across one after the zombie apocalypse has begun.

Be creative! What common objects could you use to defend yourself?

The best weapons are easy to **WIELD**, light, and able to clear any number of zombies out of your path. Such weapons include gardening tools (shovels and rakes), kitchen supplies (rolling pins and frying pans), and sports equipment (baseball bats and tennis rackets). These are the best weapons because they will be easy to find in the zombie apocalypse when you're fleeing from brain-hungry zombies all the time. Sure, a shotgun would probably be more useful than a shovel, but you aren't going to find many. So, by all means keep your eyes peeled for bazookas, but make sure you practice fighting with a frying pan in the meantime.

BE RESOURCEFUL

When preparing to fight off an oncoming horde of undead, you can't be picky. Don't try to find the perfect weapon, just grab the nearest thing that will do the job. Small pieces of furniture, stray bits of wood, and even large stones can make decent weapons and knowing how to use them could save your life.

TOOLS

Tools are something that all survival experts rely on. Without a good set of tools, you won't get very far. Once you've set up your hideout, be sure to collect supplies and tools so that you can fortify it. The supplies you collect might also come in handy if you ever need to repair your hideout after a horde of the infected chew their way in. You're going to need wood, a hammer, and lots of nails. Any metal sheets you come across could also be used to give your hideout some extra protection. This isn't a home DIY job like re-tiling the bathroom floor — it doesn't have to look nice. All it needs to be is zombie-proof. The more nails and wood, the better.

There are also a couple of tools that will prove to be useful when you are out gathering supplies. First, a crowbar. All the wonderful automatic doors that stores have these days will be very difficult to get through once there is no more electricity. Using a crowbar, you can easily pry store doors apart and take your pick from the items within.

Another tool that is essential to surviving in the cold, dark zombie apocalypse is a flashlight. However, you must be careful. While a flashlight helps you to see in the dark, it also helps the zombies see you...

HOW TO FIGHT A ZOMBIE

The time has come to fight your first zombie. If you've been very lucky, you might have managed to get through the first few weeks without having an actual, one-on-one fight with a zombie. You might even have a well-protected hideout and a good amount of supplies at this point. If you've been less lucky, you might only just now be realizing that the zombie apocalypse has begun – as a blood-covered zombie stares at you like you're a piece of meat.

AVOID THE MOUTH

One rule is more important than all the rest when fighting a zombie – avoid the mouth. If you're bitten by a zombie during a fight, it doesn't really matter if you win or not. Once you've been bitten, you're going to turn into a zombie. That's it. Game over. You're as good as undead. So, when you're fighting your first zombie, make sure to watch its mouth and avoid being bitten at all costs. Otherwise, the first zombie you fight will also be the last.

ZOMBIES CAN'T SWIM

It's a little-known fact, but zombies can't handle water. Sure, if you pour a little water on a zombie, it's not going to help you win a fight against it. However, if you can get the zombie to fall into deep water, you've practically won the fight.

Zombies barely have the COORDINATION to walk, let alone swim. So once you've managed to trick your zombie into some deep water, such as a swimming pool, river, or pond, you can be pretty sure that it'll be stuck there splashing about forever.

TRIPPING A ZOMBIE

When fighting a zombie, keep in mind that they are immensely stupid. Zombies don't plan out their attack — they barely even look where they are going. There's a number of ways to use a zombie's stupidity against them, but one of the easiest is to trip them over. You can try using your weapons to do this, but you might get too close and end up getting nibbled. Instead, set up a TRIPWIRE or simply push things into the bumbling zombie's path. Once the zombie has fallen, you can either attack or take the chance to run away.

AIM FOR THE HEAD

If there comes a time when you can't defeat a zombie using your SUPERIOR skill and intelligence, you will have to attack it. In this situation, there is only one thing you need to know — aim for the head.

The little brain-power that zombies do have is the only thing that keeps them walking around and hunting for brains. To stop a zombie once and for all, you need to aim for its head.

SURVIVING THE ZOMBIE APOCALYPSE

If you follow this guide, then life in the zombie apocalypse might not be too bad for you. You'll have a decent hideout that is well stocked with food and supplies. You'll feel safe in the knowledge that your hideout is well protected against a zombie attack. And, should any zombies gnaw their way through the walls of your hideout, you'll know just how to fight them off.

However, life in the zombie apocalypse can be very quiet and lonely. Whether you are alone or have found a group to work with, hiding from zombies can get very boring. With only the possibility of becoming lunch for a zombie to keep you entertained, people can start to go tense. To avoid this fate, make sure that you have a hobby. Write stories, practice sports or learn an instrument, (but not too loud, as nearby zombies may hear you) — do anything that takes your mind off the apocalypse, even if it's just for a second.

GLOSSARY

BASE — a safe building that is used as headquarters for a group of people

BLOODSHOT — tinged with blood

COORDINATION — the ability to precisely use different parts of your body at the same time

FORTIFY — provide protection in case of an attack

GAIT — the way someone walks

HORDE — a large number of zombies that move in a group

IDENTIFY — spot or recognize

INFECTED — someone who has caught the zombie infection — in other words, a zombie

LOOKOUT — a person whose job it is to keep watch for zombies and danger

MAINS ELECTRICITY — the general-purpose power supply that is supplied directly to homes

PERIMETER — the outermost points or boundary of an area

SUPERIOR — higher in rank, status, authority, or ability

SURVIVAL MODE — when a person automatically starts doing whatever necessary to survive

TARGET — an object of attention or attack

TRIPWIRE — a wire stretched close to the ground that can be used to trip up a zombie

UNDEAD — someone who is dead, but is still moving around like they're alive – in other words, a zombie

WIELD — to hold and use a weapon or tool

INDEX